Anton Sunberry

THE GIRL & THE DRAGON

Illustrated by Nataliya Shevchuk

On a very cold and cloudy planet far away, there lived Laliya the Great Magician. Although she was just a little girl, Laliya had a lot of responsibilities. Everybody viewed her as a great magician and ruler, but no one thought of her as a friend. This was why she was terribly lonely, and never smiled.

Every year, Laliya's planet became cloudier and colder. Everyone expected Laliya the Great Magician to discover the spell that would return the sunshine to their planet. Therefore, from early morning till late at night, Laliya looked for a way to do this.

One night, she read about the Pyramid of Knowledge, the top of which rose above the clouds. Any magician who climbed the pyramid would have all the wisdom in the universe.

"Why doesn't this book say where this pyramid is?" exclaimed Laliya disappointedly before she continued her search.

When the girl opened the next book, a picture of a strange beast fell from it.

It would be interesting to have a closer look at this beast, Laliya thought.

There was a clap of thunder and a flash of lightning, and then a huge beast appeared in the middle of the castle library.

The beast was waving his gigantic wings, snapping his claws, and gnashing his teeth. He also started blowing so hard that the books began falling from the shelves.

"Please stop, you unknown beast!" said Laliya, strengthening her voice with the help of her magic.

As the beast bent his long neck and opened his jaws, a flame shot from its mouth and flew toward the little magician.

Laliya wasn't frightened. She deflected the fire with her magical skills.

It would be better and safer if I studied this beast outside, thought the girl. She used a spell to get out of the castle and took the dangerous beast with her.

He was now flapping his wings angrily as he hovered high above the ground, but he couldn't fly away. "Why can't I fly away? What's holding me?" roared the beast.

"I'm holding you," Laliya explained. "I'm Laliya the Great Magician. And who are you?"

"I'm a dragon," snarled the beast. "Let me go!"

"All right." The girl nodded. "Just promise to calm down."

The beast agreed and sank cautiously to the ground. "Where am I?" he asked. "How did I get here?"

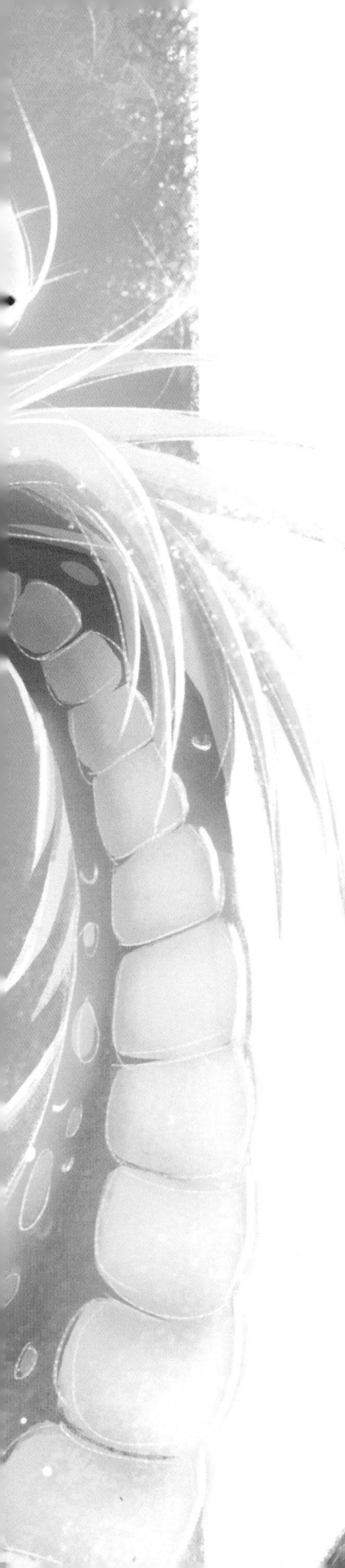

"You're on a planet called Foggytera," Laliya said. "I brought you here . . . accidentally."

"Accidentally?!" The dragon was indignant. "Send me back immediately then!"

"I'm so sorry. I don't know how to do that," the girl confessed. "But if you help me find the Pyramid of Knowledge, I'll climb it and find out everything, and then I'll be able to send you back home."

Every morning since that day, Laliya mounted the dragon, and they flew from her castle and went in search of the Pyramid of Knowledge. The dragon rose above the clouds and flew as far as the eyes could see.

Laliya was surprised. “The clouds look different from the top than from the bottom. So, that’s how it was before the clouds blocked the sun.”

When the dragon was tired, they stopped on the fluffiest cloud and began to talk.

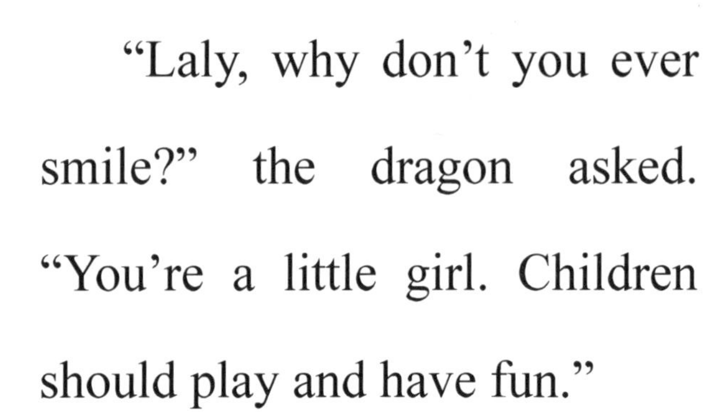

"Laly, why don't you ever smile?" the dragon asked. "You're a little girl. Children should play and have fun."

"I'm Laliya the Great Magician. I don't have time for stupidity."

"You're as boring as your cloudy planet." The dragon chuckled.

"What?!" Laliya jumped up and stamped her foot. "You have absolutely no respect for my title and our traditions!"

"Oh, that's ticklish!" the dragon yelled. "Please stop!"

"I will not stop!" Laliya began running around the dragon's belly.

The dragon laughed out loud, and his laughter was so contagious that Laliya couldn't resist smiling. Laliya the Great Magician's first smile lit up everything around them. It was as if the sun had peered out from behind the clouds.

And then something incredible happened! All the clouds that had covered Foggytera for ages suddenly moved away, and people were astonished to see the endless blue sky.

Some of them said that Laliya the Great Magician had finally found the right spell. Others said that the sun had reappeared because the Sunny Dragon had visited their planet.

The next morning, Laliya awoke to the dragon's scream. "Laly, you must see this!" he shouted from outside her window. "How can you sleep when there is such beauty?"

A few minutes later, Laliya went into the castle park and saw thousands of incredibly beautiful flowers.

She looked at them and smiled. But then she suddenly became sad.

"What's wrong?" asked the dragon. "Don't you like the flowers?"

"They are beautiful," said Laliya. "I'm just sorry that we didn't find the Pyramid of Knowledge. Thanks to you, we can all rejoice in the sun, but you're missing your home. I promise that I will definitely find this pyramid and discover a way to get you home."

"To be honest, I don't really want to go home anymore," the dragon confessed. "I have nothing important to do there and no friends either. And here I have a real friend—you, Laly. So I've decided to stay!"

"Hooray!" exclaimed Laliya joyfully, and she started laughing happily for the first time in her life.

The girl no longer needed to find the Pyramid of Knowledge; she had already gained wisdom in her heart.

If you want to learn more about the Girl and the Dragon, sign on my website,

antonsunberry.com,

and get a free gift – the printable colorings.

More by Anton Sunberry

Available at amazon

Available at amazon

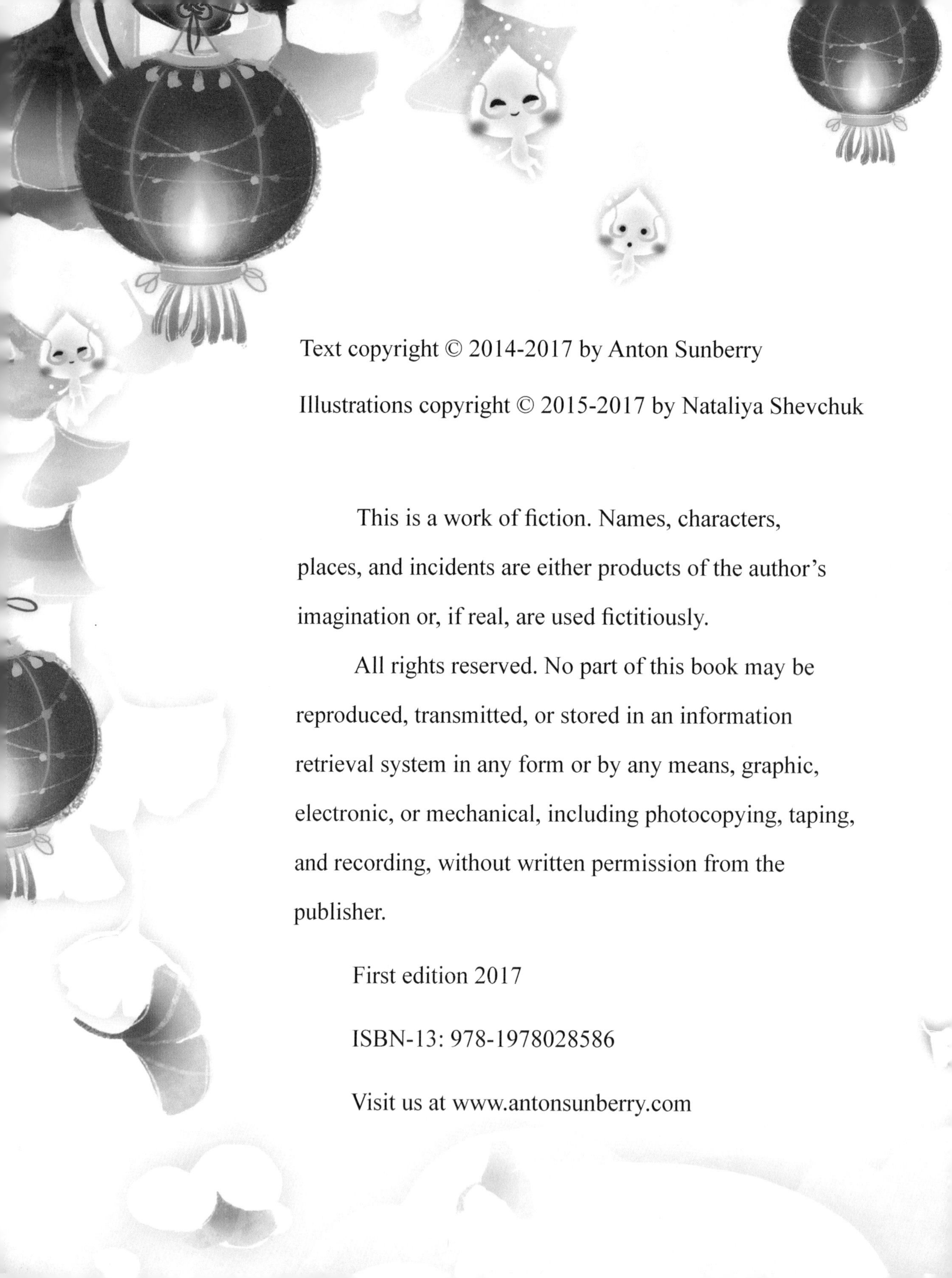

This is a work of fiction. Names, characters, places, and incidents are either products of the author's imagination or, if real, are used fictitiously.

First edition 2017

ISBN-13: 978-1978028586

Visit us at www.antonsunberry.com

Made in the USA
Columbia, SC
14 November 2017